CAPTIVE

MINDS

Table of Contents

CHAPTER 1

STRANDED

The sound of crashing waves was the first thing that greeted Jane as she slowly opened her eyes. She sat up abruptly, her head spinning as she tried to make sense of her surroundings. She was on a beach, that much was clear, but she had no idea how she had gotten there.

She looked around frantically, searching for any sign of civilization, but all she could see was sand and water as far as the eye could see. She was alone.

Panic began to set in as she scrambled to her feet, her eyes scanning the horizon for any sign of rescue. That was when she saw him. A man was lying a few yards away, his chest rising and falling in a steady rhythm.

Jane hurried over to him, her heart pounding in her chest. "Hello?" she called out, shaking his shoulder gently. "Can you hear me?"

The man's eyes fluttered open, and he groaned in confusion as he tried to sit up. "What the hell is going on?" he muttered, rubbing his head.

Jane could see the fear and confusion in his eyes, and it mirrored her own feelings. "I don't know," she said, her voice shaking. "I woke up here, and I have no memory of how I got here."

The man looked around, taking in their surroundings for the first time. "Where the hell are we?" he said his voice tight with panic.

Jane shook her head. "I don't know," she repeated. "But we need to find out and fast."

The two strangers looked at each other warily. They were both feeling a sense of distrust and uncertainty, not knowing what the future holds.

As they tried to stand up, they both noticed that they were wearing matching bracelets on their wrists. It was strange, they didn't remember putting them on, but they both had the same one.

"Do you remember anything?" the man asked, looking at the bracelet on his wrist.

"No," Jane said, "I don't remember anything. Do you?"

The man shook his head. "No, I don't remember anything either."

They both stood there for a moment, looking at each other and realizing that they were in this together. They started to explore the island, looking for any sign of civilization or rescue. But as the hours passed and the sun began to set, it became clear that they were truly stranded.

As they settled down for the night, huddled together for warmth and comfort, they could only hope that they would find a way off the island before it was too late.

The night was long and restless for Jane and the stranger. They took turns keeping watch, unsure of what dangers might lurk on the island. As dawn broke, they decided to continue their search for a way off the island.

As they walked, they came across a small stream, providing them with fresh water to drink. They also found a cave that offered shelter from the sun. They decided to rest there and take stock of their supplies.

Jane rummaged through her pockets and found a small flashlight, a lighter and a pocket knife. The man had a water bottle, a compass and a small first aid kit. They shared the supplies and discussed their options.

"We need to find a way to signal for help," the man said, looking out at the ocean. "But I don't think we have enough supplies to last more than a few days."

Jane nodded, her stomach twisting with worry. "We need to find a way to make a fire," she said. "Maybe someone will see the smoke."

The man nodded, and they set to work gathering dry wood and leaves to make a fire. It took them several tries, but they finally managed to get a small flame going.

As they sat by the fire, they could both sense a growing sense of unease. They had no idea how they had gotten to the island or what their fate would be. They both knew that time was running out, and they needed to find a way off the island before it was too late.

As the sun began to set, they decided to call it a day, and they settled down for another night. They knew that the next day would bring new challenges, and they would have to be ready for anything.

As they drifted off to sleep, they could only hope that they would be rescued before it was too late. The uncertainty of their fate weighed heavily on them, but they knew that they had to stay strong and keep fighting for survival.

CHAPTER 2

CLUES

The next day, Jane and the stranger set out early to continue their search for answers. They had woken up with a renewed sense of determination and a feeling that they were getting closer to the truth.

As they walked, they noticed that the island was not as deserted as they had first thought. They came across various signs of human activity, such as footprints and discarded items, which sparked hope that they were not alone on the island.

Their path led them to a dense jungle, where they had to hack their way through the thick underbrush with their pocket knives. The jungle was teeming with life, and they could hear the calls of exotic birds and the rustling of unseen animals.

As they pushed deeper into the jungle, they came across a clearing. In the center of the clearing stood a large stone structure, covered in moss and vines. They approached it cautiously, unsure of what they might find.

As they drew closer, they could see that the structure was some sort of temple. There were carvings and symbols on the walls that neither of them could decipher. They explored the temple, finding a small room at the back that contained a stone table and several artifacts.

One of the artifacts caught their attention. It was a small metal box, intricately decorated with symbols that matched those on the temple walls. The stranger managed to open the box, and inside they found a small journal.

The journal was filled with notes and drawings, and it quickly became clear that it belonged to someone who had been studying the island and the temple for a long time. They read through the journal, their hearts pounding with excitement as they began to piece together the truth.

The journal revealed that the island had been used by a mysterious organization for secret experiments and that the temple was the key to unlocking the secrets of the island. The journal also contained a map of the island, indicating that there was a hidden laboratory somewhere on the island.

As they read the journal, they realized that they had been brought to the island for a purpose. They were part of the organization's experiment, and they needed to find the laboratory and uncover the truth about their captivity.

They quickly gathered up the journal and the other artifacts, and they set out to follow the map. They knew that time was running out, and they had to find the laboratory before it was too late.

As they walked, they were both filled with a sense of unease, but also a sense of purpose. They were getting closer to the truth, and they were determined to uncover it, no matter what the cost.

As they walked, they came across more signs of human activity, such as discarded equipment and tools. They knew they were getting closer to the laboratory.

They soon found a narrow path that led into a steep incline. They climbed it carefully, their hearts pounding with excitement and fear. At the top of the incline, they found a small plateau. And there, nestled in a clearing, was the laboratory.

It was a large, modern building, surrounded by a fence and cameras. They approached it cautiously, unsure of what they would find inside.

As they entered the laboratory, they were greeted by a sterile, antiseptic environment. They could see rows of lab tables, computers, and equipment. But there was no one in sight.

They began to explore the lab, looking for any clues that might help them understand their captivity. They found a series of notes and reports, detailing the organization's experiments on the island. They also found several artifacts, similar to the ones they had found in the temple.

As they studied the notes and artifacts, they began to piece together the truth. They realized that the organization had been experimenting with mind control, using the artifacts and the temple to manipulate the subjects of their experiments.

"This is insane," Jane said, her voice shaking with anger. "They've been using us for their experiments. We have to put a stop to this."

The stranger nodded, his jaw set with determination. "We need to find out more about this organization and who is behind it," he said. "We can't let them get away with this."

They continued to search the lab, looking for any information that might help them in their quest for the truth. They found a computer that contained files and information about the organization and its members. They also found a communication system, which they used to try and contact the outside world.

As they worked, they could both sense a growing sense of urgency. They knew that they had to find a way off the island and reveal the truth about the organization and its experiments. They were determined to put a stop to it, no matter what the cost.

They spent the rest of the day analyzing the information they had found and making a plan. They knew that time was running out, and they had to act fast if they wanted to escape the island and reveal the truth.

As night fell, they settled down in the lab to rest. They were exhausted from their long day of exploration and analysis. However, their rest was short-lived as they soon heard a loud noise coming from outside the lab.

They quickly grabbed their supplies and hid in the shadows, unsure of what was happening. They soon realized that they were not alone on the island. They saw several men, armed and dressed in black, approaching the lab.

They realized that they had been discovered and that they were in grave danger. They knew they had to act fast if they wanted to survive.

Jane suggested that they could use the lab's equipment to their advantage. They quickly set up a makeshift alarm system using the lab's equipment, linking it to the communication system. They also set up a trap using chemicals and equipment found in the lab.

The armed men entered the lab, but the alarm went off, and the trap was triggered, causing a chemical reaction that created a thick smoke, blinding the intruders. While they were distracted, Jane and the stranger managed to slip past them and make a run for it.

They ran as fast as they could, dodging trees and underbrush, their hearts pounding with fear. They could hear the men shouting and chasing after them, but they managed to stay ahead of them.

Finally, they reached the beach, where they had first awakened. They could see a boat approaching the shore. They recognized it as the boat of the mysterious organization that had brought them to the island.

They rushed into the water, swimming out to the boat as fast as they could. They managed to climb aboard, and they quickly set sail, leaving the island and the armed men behind.

As they sailed away, they could both sense a sense of relief and triumph. They had managed to escape the island and uncover the truth about the organization and its experiments. They knew that their journey was far from over, and they would have to continue to fight to reveal the truth and bring those responsible to justice.

The laboratory was a large modern building, with a metal and glass exterior, surrounded by a fence and cameras. Inside, it was a sterile, antiseptic environment, with rows of lab tables, computers, and equipment. The equipment was state of the art and well-maintained. They could see that the laboratory was used for scientific research and experimentation. They found several notes and reports, detailing the organization's experiments on the island, as well as several artifacts that were similar to the ones they had found in the temple. They also found a computer that contained files and information about the organization and its members. They could see that the laboratory was the center of the organization's operations on the island, and it was from where they controlled the experiments and the subjects.

CHAPTER 3
CAPTURED

As Jane and the stranger sailed away from the island, they felt a sense of relief and triumph. They had managed to escape the island and uncover the truth about the organization and its experiments. They knew that their journey was far from over, and they would have to continue to fight to reveal the truth and bring those responsible to justice.

However, their relief was short-lived as they soon discovered that they had unknowingly triggered the ship's alarm system. They realized too late that the boat they had boarded was not a rescue boat but an escape boat for the organization's members.

As the night passed, the alarm attracted the attention of other ships in the area, and by morning, they found themselves surrounded by a fleet of ships belonging to the organization. They were now forcefully rather than deceptively captivated.

As they were boarded and taken into custody, they could both sense a feeling of hopelessness and despair. They had come so close to freedom, only to be caught once again.

They were taken to a large ship, where they were interrogated and questioned about their knowledge of the organization and its experiments. They were also searched and their findings and artifacts were confiscated.

As they were being questioned, they could see the fear and uncertainty in the eyes of the organization members, they knew they were not the only ones who were being used as pawns in their game.

Despite their captors' threats and intimidation, Jane and the stranger refused to give up the information they had uncovered. They knew that the truth needed to be revealed, and they would do whatever it takes to ensure that it was.

As the night passed, they were thrown into a cell, with no idea of what the future held. They were determined to find a way to escape and continue their quest for the truth, but they knew that it would not be easy. They were now in the hands of the very organization they were trying to expose, and their future was uncertain.

As the night passed, Jane and the stranger were thrown into a small cell, with no idea of what the future held. They huddled together for warmth and comfort, trying to come up with a plan.

"We have to find a way out of here," Jane whispered, her voice filled with determination. "We can't let them win."

"I know," the stranger replied, his jaw set with determination. "We have to keep fighting. We can't give up now."

They were interrupted by the sound of a door opening, and a man walked in. He was tall, with piercing blue eyes and a cold, calculating expression. He was dressed in an expensive suit, and it was clear that he was the owner of the organization.

"Welcome to my ship," the man said, his voice cold and emotionless. "I see you've been busy, discovering the truth about my organization and its experiments."

Jane and the stranger looked at each other, fear and anger in their eyes. They knew that this man was responsible for their captivity and the experiments on the island.

"Why?" Jane asked, her voice shaking with anger. "Why did you do this? Why did you use us for your experiments?"

The man chuckled, a cold, cruel sound.

"Why? Because it's all about power and control," the man said, a hint of madness in his voice. "My organization has been experimenting with mind control and manipulation, using the artifacts and the temple on the island to control the subjects of our experiments. And you, my dear subjects, were the perfect test subjects for our latest project."

The stranger's face twisted with disgust. "You're sick," he said, his voice filled with contempt. "You have no right to play God with people's lives like this."

The man's expression turned to one of anger. "I have every right," he said. "I am the one in control here. And you will do as I say, or suffer the consequences."

Jane could see the fear and anger in the stranger's eyes, and she knew that they had to find a way out of this situation. She tried to keep a brave face, not wanting to show the man how much he was getting to her.

"What do you want from us?" she asked her voice steady.

The man's expression softened and a sly smile spread across his face. "I want you to continue to be my test subjects," he said. "I have big plans for my organization, and I need subjects like you to help me achieve my goals

Jane agrees to the demands and she persuades the stranger to play along after the man had left

Jane's mind was racing as the man spoke. She knew that they were in a dangerous situation and that they had to find a way out of it. She knew that they had to play along with the man's demands, at least for now.

"Alright," she said her voice calm and steady. "We'll do as you say. But you have to promise that you'll let us go once your experiments are over."

The man's expression turned to one of satisfaction. "Of course," he said. "Once our experiments are complete, you'll be free to go."

With that, he turned and left the cell, leaving Jane and the stranger alone.

As soon as the man was gone, Jane turned to the stranger. "We have to play along with him," she said, her voice low. "We have to find a way to escape and stop this madness."

The stranger nodded, understanding the gravity of the situation. "We'll do whatever it takes," he said. "We can't let him get away with this."

They spent the rest of the night coming up with a plan, determined to escape and bring the organization and its experiments to light. They knew that it wouldn't be easy, but they were willing to risk everything to stop the organization and its cruel experiments once and for all.

As they continued to plan their escape, Jane found herself struggling to remember John's name. She knew it was important to know his name, especially if they were going to work together to escape.

"What was your name again?" she asked, trying to keep her voice steady.

John looked at her, a hint of amusement in his eyes. "It's John," he said, trying to help her out.

Jane felt a wave of embarrassment wash over her. "I'm sorry, I should have remembered," she said, feeling foolish.

John shook his head, his expression kind. "It's alright, we're under a lot of stress," he reassured her. "It's important that we focus on the plan and getting out of here. We'll worry about names later."

Jane nodded, grateful for John's understanding. They continued to plan and strategize, determined to escape and bring the organization and its cruel experiments to light. They knew that it wouldn't be easy, but they were willing to risk everything to stop the organization and its cruel experiments once and for all.

CHAPTER 4

COLD POWER

Jane and John were taken back to the laboratory, but this time they were brought to a room that they had never seen before. As they entered, they were startled to see past subjects hanging all around the room, with wires and tubes connected to their bodies. They were all lifeless, their eyes staring blankly ahead.

Jane and John could feel their blood running cold as they realized what was happening. They were horrified by the sight of the subjects, who were being used as a power source for the laboratory.

"What is this?" Jane exclaimed, her voice trembling with anger. "What have you done to these people?"

The man who had brought them to the room turned to them, a cold, calculating expression on his face. "These people are the power source for the laboratory," he said, his voice cold and emotionless. "They are providing the energy needed to keep the lab running."

John's face twisted with disgust. "You're using them as a power source?" he said, his voice filled with contempt. "That's monstrous!"

The man shrugged, unfazed by their reactions. "It's necessary," he said. "Without a power source, the laboratory would not be able to function."

Jane and John could hardly believe what they were hearing. They had never imagined that the organization would stoop to such lows. They knew they had to find a way out of this situation, and fast.

"What about us?" Jane asked, her voice shaking with anger. "Are you going to use us for the power source too?"

The man smiled a cold, cruel smile. "You'll be next," he said, his voice filled with menace. "You'll be providing the energy needed to keep the lab running."

Jane and John could both sense a feeling of hopelessness and despair. They knew that they had to find a way out of this situation before it was too late. They had to stop the organization and its cruel experiments once and for all. They had to find a way to escape before they too became the power source for the laboratory.

Jane and John were moved to a clearing at the back of the laboratory, where they were strapped to chairs and fitted with a special headset. They could see that the clearing was surrounded by tall trees, and the sky was overcast, matching the gloomy atmosphere of the situation.

As the man and his staff prepared for the mind control test, Jane and John could sense a feeling of hopelessness and despair. They knew that they had to find a way out of this situation before it was too late.

The man approached them, a cold, calculating expression on his face. "Welcome to the final stage of our experiment," he said, his voice cold and emotionless. "You will be subjected to a mind control test using this special headset. You will be under our complete control, and you will do as we say."

Jane and John could see the fear and uncertainty in the eyes of the organization members; they knew they were not the only ones who were being used as pawns in their game.

CHAPTER 5
CONTROLLED

As the test began, Jane and John could feel a strange sensation in their heads, as if their thoughts were being manipulated. They could hear the man's voice in their heads, telling them to obey his commands.

They tried to fight back, but it was as if their minds were trapped in a battle. They could feel the headset's effects taking over, but they didn't give up. They tried to remember who they were, and that they were not puppets to be controlled by anyone.

The weather outside reflected the struggle within their minds, the sky was darkening, and the wind was picking up, a storm was brewing.

As the test continued, the man and his staff observed Jane and John's reactions, taking notes and making adjustments to the headset's settings. They could see that the subjects were resisting the mind control, but they were determined to make it work.

Finally, after what felt like an eternity, Jane and John managed to break free from the mind control. They could feel a sense of relief and triumph. They had managed to resist the mind control, and they knew that they had to use this opportunity to escape and bring the organization and its experiments to light.

As they struggle to break free of the bindings and the headset, they could hear the man's voice ordering his staff to stop them, but they were determined to escape, no matter the cost.

As the test was deemed successful, the man and his staff injected a sedative directly into Jane and John's head, weakening them and making it easier to control their actions. Their first task was to scurry the island and find some food.

Jane's mind was in turmoil, as she realized that she no longer had control over her body. She could feel the sedative taking over, making it difficult to think and reason. Inside her head, she started a conversation with herself, trying to come up with a plan.

"I can't let them control me," she thought. "I have to find a way out of this situation. I have to fight back."

She tried to focus her thoughts, to remember who she was and what she stood for. She knew that she had to find a way to escape and bring the organization and its experiments to light.

As she walked through the island, searching for food, she tried to keep her mind clear, to look for any opportunity to escape. She knew that she had to be careful, as the man and his staff were watching her every move.

She spent hours searching the island, her mind racing as she tried to come up with a plan. She knew that time was running out, and she had to act fast.

Finally, as dusk fell, she returned to the clearing, where she found John waiting for her. They could both see the determination in each other's eyes, and they knew that they had to find a way out of this situation, and fast.

As the days passed, Jane and John were subjected to several more tests, each one more difficult and intense than the last. They were forced to perform tasks and obey commands, all under the control of the mind control headset.

Despite the challenges, they were both determined to regain control over their minds and bodies. They spent their nights in the cell discussing their experiences, trying to understand what was happening to them.

"I can't believe they're doing this to us," Jane said, her voice filled with anger. "We have to find a way out of this situation."

"I know," John replied; his jaw set with determination. "We have to keep fighting. We can't give up now."

As the tests continued, they both started to notice small changes. They were able to resist the mind control for longer periods of time, and they could feel a sense of control returning to their minds.

"I think we're getting stronger," John said, hope in his voice. "We're starting to regain control."

"I agree," Jane said, her eyes shining with determination. "We have to keep fighting. We can't let them control us forever."

They both knew that it would not be easy, but they were determined to escape and bring the organization and its experiments to light. They knew that their future was uncertain, but they were willing to risk everything to stop the organization and its cruel experiments once and for all.

"I can't believe they're still doing this to us," Jane said, her voice filled with anger and frustration. "We've been here for what feels like forever, and they're still running these experiments on us."

John shook his head in agreement, "It's been an endless cycle of tests and trials, it's like they're trying to break us."

Jane leaned back against the wall of the cell, "I keep trying to remember who I was before all of this, but it's like my memories are slipping away."

John reached out and took her hand, "We have to hold on to who we are, that's the only way we can fight back against them."

Jane turned to John with a determined look in her eyes, "You're right, we can't let them control us. We have to find a way out of here, we have to stop them."

John nodded, "We'll figure it out together, and we'll find a way. But we have to be patient; we can't rush into anything without a plan."

Jane took a deep breath, "Okay, let's think this through. We need to find out more about their operations, gather information, and look for weaknesses in their security."

John nodded in agreement, "It's been an endless cycle of tests and trials, it's like they're trying to break us. I've been trying to resist the mind control, but it's hard when they keep adjusting the headset."

Jane leaned back against the wall of the cell, "I keep trying to remember who I was before all of this, but it's like my memories are slipping away. I can't even remember my family's faces anymore."

John reached out and took her hand, "We have to hold on to who we are, that's the only way we can fight back against them. I remember the first time they put that headset on me, I couldn't even move my own body, and it was like I was trapped in my own mind."

Jane squeezed his hand, "We'll get through this together, and we have to. We can't let them control us anymore, we have to find a way out of here and put a stop to this."

John looked at her with determination, "You're right, we have to make a plan. We'll gather information, look for weaknesses in their security, and find a way to escape."

They sat in silence for a moment, both lost in thought as they planned their next move. They knew that it wouldn't be easy, but they were determined to escape and bring the organization and its cruel experiments to light.

CHAPTER 6

BROKEN

The next day, something unexpected happened that completely changed the course of Jane and John's situation. As they were being led to another round of tests, Jane noticed something strange about John's behavior. He seemed to be too familiar with the guards and the laboratory, as if he had been there before.

Jane started to pay close attention to John's actions and behavior, and soon, she found strong evidence that he was one of the workers for the mysterious organization. She noticed that he knew the layout of the laboratory and the routines of the guards too well. He also had detailed knowledge of the experiments and the technology being used.

Jane was shocked and heartbroken at this revelation. She couldn't believe that John, who she had trusted and confided in, was actually one of the people responsible for her captivity and the cruel experiments.

She confronted John about her suspicions, and he didn't deny it. He revealed that he was indeed one of the workers for the organization and that he had been tasked with keeping an eye on her and the other subjects.

Jane was devastated, she felt betrayed and used. She didn't know who she could trust anymore and felt alone in her struggle against the organization. She knew she had to find a way to escape and bring the organization and its experiments to light, but now she had to do it alone.

Jane was in tears as she confronted John about her suspicions. "How could you do this to me?" she cried, her voice filled with heartbreak. "I trusted you, I confided in you, and all this time you were one of them?"

John tried to explain that it wasn't true, that he had been planted by the organization to keep an eye on her and the other subjects, but she wouldn't listen. She was too hurt and angry to hear his explanation.

"You're just like them," she said, her voice filled with disdain. "You used me and played me for a fool. I can't even look at you right now."

John tried to reach out to her, but she pushed him away, her heart heavy with betrayal. She walked out of the cell, leaving John behind.

As she submitted to the tests, she couldn't shake off the feeling of betrayal and hurt. She knew that she had to focus on her escape and bringing the organization and its experiments to light, but it was hard to do when she felt so alone. She couldn't trust anyone, not even the person she had thought was her ally.

The experience left her with a deep feeling of mistrust and skepticism. She couldn't trust anyone easily and would have to be careful with who she confides in the future. Her determination to escape and bring the organization to light however remained undeterred.

During one of the tests, the organization decided to simulate a scene in Jane's mind of a friendly conversation between the owner of the company and John. They wanted to see how she would react and if it would break her spirit. In this simulated scene, the owner of the company is praising John for his work and thanking him for his loyalty while John is smiling and nodding in agreement.

Jane's mind was filled with pain and betrayal as she watched this scene play out in her mind. She couldn't believe that John would betray her and side with her captors. She cried uncontrollably, her heart breaking as she watched the scene unfold.

John, who was also being subjected to the test, could see what was happening to Jane. He could see the pain and betrayal on her face and knew that the scene was not real. He tried to scream out to her, to tell her that it was just a simulation, but his voice was muffled by the soundproof glass booth where he was being held.

The organization observed Jane's reaction with satisfaction; they were pleased to see that the simulation had the desired effect on her. However, John was filled with rage and frustration as he watched Jane cry her eyes out; he was powerless to stop it. He knew that he had to find a way to prove his innocence and get through to her before it was too late.

The plan was to break Jane and force her to stop trying to escape. Reveal this in a conversation between the owner and his staff in the booth were John was held

The owner of the organization and his staff watched Jane's reaction with satisfaction from the soundproof glass booth where John was being held.

"Excellent work, the simulation had the desired effect," the owner said, a hint of a smile on his face. "She's broken; she'll stop trying to escape now."

One of the staff members nodded, "Yes, the plan worked perfectly. We were able to weaken her resolve and make her doubt her own memories."

Another staff member added, "We also managed to turn her against her ally, it'll be easier to control her now that she's isolated."

The owner nodded, "Good, now we can focus on the next phase of the experiment. We'll see how long it takes before she fully submits to our control."

John listened in horror as the owner and his staff discussed their plan to break Jane and force her to stop trying to escape. He knew that he had to find a way to prove his innocence and get through to Jane before it was too late. He couldn't let them control her and use her for their twisted experiments. He had to find a way to escape and put a stop to the organization's cruel actions once and for all.

As Jane and John were put back in their cell, they sat silently apart from each other. Jane was curled up in a corner, her face buried in her hands as she cried. John could see the pain and betrayal etched on her face.

He tried to explain to her that the simulation was not real, that he had never betrayed her, but she wouldn't listen. It seemed that the company's mind control was working even without all the gadgets attached to her. She was too hurt and angry to hear him out.

John knew that he had to find a different way to help her out. He couldn't let her continue to suffer like this, he had to find a way to break through the mind control and prove his innocence.

He spent the next days trying to come up with a plan, but it was difficult with the constant surveillance and the lack of resources. He knew that he had to be careful and not to let the guards suspect anything.

He also tried to reach out to Jane, but she still refused to listen or talk to him, it seemed the mind control had done a number on her and was still affecting her. John knew that time was running out and he had to act fast. He couldn't let the organization continue to control and use them for their twisted experiments. He had to find a way to escape and put a stop to it once and for all.

After several days of thinking and planning, John finally discovered a way to break Jane out of the mind control. He realized that the best way to do it was by playing along with the organization's plan and leading Jane far away from the laboratory. He hoped that once they were away from the source of the mind control, the effect would wear off and she would be able to regain her freedom of thought.

John knew that this plan was risky and that there were many factors that could go wrong, but he was determined to save Jane and put a stop to the organization's cruel experiments. He spent the next few days carefully laying the groundwork for his plan. He pretended to continue going along with the organization's tests and commands, all the while, gathering information and looking for a way to escape.

He also tried to reach out to Jane, to let her know that he was still on her side and that he was working to save her. He knew it would be difficult for her to trust him again, but he hoped that once the mind control was gone, she would understand and forgive him.

John's plan was not easy and had many obstacles, but he was determined to save Jane, he knew that he had to act fast and he couldn't let the organization continue to control and use them for their twisted experiments. He had to find a way to escape and put a stop to it once and for all.

John knew that it was time to execute his plan, and he had to act fast before it was too late. He waited for the next round of tests and when the opportunity presented itself, he put his plan into action.

He pretended to be fully under the organization's control and acted rough towards Jane, pushing her and shouting commands in order to make her move in the direction he wanted. He knew that it would be hard for her to trust him, especially after the simulation that the organization had implanted in her mind, but he hoped that she would understand that he was doing this for her own good.

He led her out of the laboratory and into the wilderness, where the mind control signal was weaker. He hoped that by getting her away from the source of the mind control, the effect would wear off and she would regain her freedom of thought.

The journey was difficult and dangerous, and Jane struggled to trust John, but he kept pushing her forward, always with the goal of freeing her from the mind control in mind. He knew that the longer they stayed in the laboratory, the harder it would be to break free.

After a few days of traveling, they finally reached a safe distance from the laboratory, and the mind control signal had worn off. Jane was finally free from the control and was able to regain her freedom of thought. She was able to understand that John was working to save her and forgive him for his actions. They were finally free and able to put a stop to the organization's cruel experiments.

After several hours of traveling, Jane and John finally reached a safe distance from the laboratory, and the mind control signal had worn off. Jane was finally free from the control and was able to regain her freedom of thought. She was able to understand that John was working to save her and forgive him for his actions. They were finally free and able to put a stop to the organization's cruel experiments.

As they sat that night, they discussed what they should do next.

"We can't just leave this place to continue its twisted experiments," Jane said, her voice filled with determination. "We have to put a stop to it once and for all."

John nodded in agreement, "I know. But how? We're just two people against a powerful organization."

"We could go to the authorities," Jane suggested. "We have proof of what they're doing here."

John shook his head, "I don't think that's the best idea. They have connections and influence, they'll just cover it up and we'll be silenced."

Jane thought for a moment and then said, "We have to destroy the laboratory and all the evidence. We have to set it on fire."

John looked at her, surprised. "Are you sure that's what you want to do?"

"Yes," Jane said firmly. "It's the only way to make sure that they can never use it again."

John thought for a moment and then nodded, "Alright, let's do it. But we have to be careful and make sure we don't get caught."

They spent the next few days planning and gathering materials they needed to set the laboratory on fire. On the night of the raid, they snuck into the laboratory, set

CHAPTER 7

UNFORTUNATE

They noticed that the organization had set out to find them. They knew that they had to act fast and come up with a plan.

John quickly came up with an idea, "We'll make it look like we got caught trying to escape. We'll entangle ourselves in some twigs and ropes and pretend that we've been trapped here."

Jane looked at him, surprised. "Are you sure that will work?"

"It's worth a shot," John said, his voice filled with determination.

They quickly put their plan into action, entangling themselves in the twigs and ropes, making it look like they had been caught trying to escape.

It wasn't long before they heard the sound of armed men approaching. The organization had found them. The men in black, armed with guns, surrounded them, their expressions cold and menacing.

"What are you doing here?" one of the men demanded, his voice filled with suspicion.

John quickly explained, "We got trapped here while trying to escape. We were caught in these twigs and ropes, we couldn't move."

The men in black looked at them skeptically but ultimately believed them. They were taken to a different part of the laboratory where they would be held till further notice.

Jane and John knew that they were lucky to be alive and were grateful for their quick thinking. They were determined to find a way to escape and bring the organization to justice.

Jane and John were taken to a different part of the laboratory where they were held until further notice. They were locked in a small room with no windows and only a single door for entrance and exit. The room was dimly lit and had a musty smell. The walls were made of concrete and the floor was cold and hard. They knew that they had to act fast and find a way to escape before it was too late.

They started looking around the room for anything that could help them escape. They noticed a control panel on the wall and they decided to take a closer look. They started messing with the controls, trying to figure out how they worked. They were determined to find a way out of there.

As they were messing with the controls, they noticed that the building started to smoke. They realized that they had accidentally set off a fire alarm. They knew that they had to act fast before the organization realized what was happening. They continued to mess with the controls, trying to find a way to escape.

As the smoke started to fill the room, they heard the sound of alarms blaring and people running in the hallway. They knew that they had to act fast before the organization realized what was happening.

The smoke was getting thicker, making it hard to see or breathe. They could hear the sound of people shouting and running in the hallway. They knew that they had to act fast before the organization realized what was happening.

They finally found the control that would open the door, and they quickly made their escape. They ran through the smoke-filled hallway, coughing and gasping for air. They could hear the sound of people shouting and running in the hallway. They knew that they had to act fast before the organization realized what was happening.

Finally, they reached the exit, and they pushed open the door and ran out of the building. They were met by the sight of the laboratory in flames, with smoke and fire everywhere. They knew that they had finally succeeded in destroying the organization's laboratory and putting a stop to their twisted experiments. They looked at each other with relief and satisfaction as they made their escape.

As Jane and John were making their escape, they could see the laboratory owner still inside the building, refusing to leave. He was crying and shouting about all the work and money that had been put into the place. They could see the desperation and sadness in his eyes, but they knew that they couldn't let him continue with his twisted experiments.

As they were watching from a distance, they heard a loud explosion, and the laboratory was engulfed in flames. They could see the laboratory owner still inside, consumed by the fire.

John quickly pulled Jane close, shielding her with his body, protecting her from the heat and debris that came flying their way. They both felt the heat and the force of the explosion, but they were safe thanks to John's quick thinking and protective actions.

As the fire and smoke cleared, they could see that the laboratory was completely destroyed and that the organization's twisted experiments had finally come to an end. They knew that it was a high price to pay, but they were relieved that they were able to put a stop to it and save countless lives in the process.

They looked at each other, both filled with relief and sadness for the loss of life, but also knowing that they had succeeded in their mission. They knew that they had to leave the place and start a new life, free from the organization and the mind control, but they would always remember the sacrifices they had to make to get there.

CHAPTER 8

EXTRACTED

They start moving west of the island back to where they first met. Helicopters began to arrive on the island and one of them landed close to them. A CIA agent steps down in full regalia

After the laboratory had been destroyed, Jane and John knew that they had to leave the island as soon as possible. They decided to head west, back to where they had first met. They knew that it was a long journey, but they were determined to make it.

As they were making their way through the wilderness, they heard the sound of helicopters in the distance. They knew that the organization would be looking for them and they had to be careful.

As they were approaching the area where they first met, they saw a helicopter landing nearby. A tall, well-built man dressed in a suit stepped out of the helicopter. He had a badge on his chest that read "CIA" and he was carrying a weapon.

The man walked towards them, his expression serious. "Jane and John, I presume?" he said, his voice deep and commanding.

Jane and John looked at each other, surprised. They had not expected to be found by the CIA.

"Yes, that's us," John said, his voice filled with uncertainty.

The man smiled, "My name is Agent Smith. I've been sent here to extract you and bring you back to the United States for debriefing."

Jane and John were relieved to hear that they were finally going to be safe and away from the organization. They knew that it was a long and hard journey, but they were grateful that it had all come to an end.

They were loaded into the helicopter and were flown back to the United States, where they were debriefed and had to explain everything that had happened to them on the island. They knew that it would be a long process, but they were glad that it was all over, and they were finally free.

As the helicopter flew back to the United States, Agent Smith began a conversation with Jane and John. He explained to them that the owner of the organization had been wanted by the CIA for the past 16 years. Despite many people having escaped and telling their stories, no one had been able to find the location of the laboratory and put a stop to the organization's twisted experiments.

"You have no idea how long we've been looking for that place," Agent Smith said, shaking his head in disbelief. "We've had so many leads, but we've never been able to find it until now."

Jane and John looked at each other, surprised. They had never imagined that their actions would have such a significant impact.

"It's all thanks to you two," Agent Smith continued. "You stood up for justice and put a stop to their evil experiments. You're true heroes."

Jane and John were filled with a sense of pride and accomplishment. They knew that they had made a difference and that their actions had saved countless lives.

"It was the fire and explosion that attracted our attention," Agent Smith said, "We couldn't have done it without you."

Jane and John knew that it was a long and hard journey, but they were glad that it had all come to an end. They were finally free and they knew that they had made a difference in the world.

As the conversation with Agent Smith continued, Jane and John noticed a change in his countenance. He reached into his pocket and pulled out a small box. He opened the box and pulled out a small badge with the CIA logo on it.

"I want to offer you both a job," Agent Smith said, his voice serious. "We would love to have you as undercover agents for the CIA."

Jane and John were shocked. They had never imagined that they would be offered a job with the CIA.

"Of course, there will be a period of internship," Agent Smith continued. "We'll need to train you and make sure you're ready for the job."

Jane and John looked at each other, unsure of what to say. They had never imagined that their actions would lead to a job offer with the CIA.

"It's an opportunity of a lifetime," Agent Smith said, "You'll be doing something important, making a difference in the world, and keeping people safe."

After hearing the agent's explanation, they both accepted the offer. They knew that it would be a long and hard journey, but they were excited for

the opportunity to make a difference in the world
and keep people safe.

CHAPTER 9
NEW LIFE

As the helicopter landed, they stepped out, ready for their new journey as CIA agents. They knew that it would be a long and hard journey, but they were ready for it, knowing that they had each other's back and that they would make a difference in the world.

After completing their internship and training, Jane and John officially became CIA agents. They were assigned to different teams and went undercover to infiltrate different organizations and stop any illegal activities. They were able to use the skills and knowledge they gained on the island to help them in their new roles.

They were able to put a stop to several illegal operations and save countless lives. They were proud of their work and were glad that they were making a difference in the world.

Despite their busy schedules and dangerous missions, they always made time to catch up and reminisce about their time on the island. They knew that they would never forget the experiences they had and the sacrifices they made.

Years passed and they both retired from the CIA as seasoned agents. They decided to move to a quiet place by the beach where they can watch the sunset and remember the past. They knew that they had lived a fulfilling life, and they were proud of the difference they had made in the world.

The end of their journey together was not the end of their story but the beginning of a new one.

They knew that they would always have each other's back, no matter what the future holds. And together, they would continue to make a difference in the world.

THE END